*Other books in this series:*
The Crazy World of Aerobics (Bill Stott)
The Crazy World of Cats (Bill Stott)
The Crazy World of Cricket (Bill Stott)
The Crazy World of Gardening (Bill Stott)
The Crazy World of Golf (Mike Scott)
The Crazy World of the Greens (Barry Knowles)
The Crazy World of the Handyman (Roland Fiddy)
The Crazy World of Hospitals (Bill Stott)
The Crazy World of Housework (Bill Stott)
The Crazy World of Love (Roland Fiddy)
The Crazy World of Marriage (Bill Stott)
The Crazy World of the Office (Bill Stott)
The Crazy World of Photography (Bill Stott)
The Crazy World of Rugby (Bill Stott)
The Crazy World of Sailing (Peter Rigby)
The Crazy World of Sex (David Pye)

Published simultaneously in 1993 by Exley Publications Ltd. in Great
Britain, and Exley Giftbooks in the USA.


Copyright © Bill Stott, 1993

ISBN 1-85015-348-5

Printed and bound by Grafo S.A., Bilbao, Spain.

Exley Publications Ltd, 16 Chalk Hill, Watford, Herts WD1 4BN,
United Kingdom.
Exley Giftbooks, 359 East Main Street, Suite 3D, Mount Kisco,
NY 10549, USA.

# the CRAZY world of LEARNING TO DRIVE

Cartoons by
Bill Stott

**EXLEY**

MT. KISCO, NEW YORK • WATFORD, UK

*"I believe in starting with basic vehicle understanding. The round things are called wheels."*

*"You'll have to take these off for the test, you know."*

*"I think your control of the vehicle will be better with the restraint behind your head."*

*"I think you'll find we make much better progress if you sit
in the front Mr. Birdswood."*

*"Now let's see if I've got it right – mirror, pedals, steering wheel –
Oh, no - the steering wheel's the big round thing right here ..."*

*"Gosh! So much to learn. Why don't you do the pedals and
I'll turn the steering thing?*

"Left? That's this one, right?"

*"Couldn't you meditate before the lesson, Mr. Hardwick?*

"Yes - er, when I said go straight ahead, I meant ..."

*"Go ahead – it's your right of way."*

"*Are people staring? Not really – you did this last week.*"

*"Well fancy that – the same bend and the same lamp as last week!"*

"It's no good. Reverse is just not my gear."

*"Red, red and amber, green, amber, red. Red, red and amber, green, amber, red. It's really rather a pretty sequence, isn't it?"*

*"What are we waiting for Mr. Wainwright? Blue?"*

*"It's not really amber is it? It's more of a saffron, don't you think?"*

*"The ones on the car will be sufficient, Mr. Pratt."*

*"You don't have a lot of faith in your students do you?"*

*"Well, if it makes you feel better ..."*

*"Do you think you could put the mascot on the back seat during the test?"*

*"Now gently on the clutch ... gently ...*

*Gently!*

*GENTLY!!!"*

*"Come on Mr. Pennington, let's get it over with."*

*"This __is__ relaxed! – You should see tense."*

*"You were taught by your father and he was a cabbie I understand ..."*

*"Have you any idea why you failed your first seven tests Mrs. Piggott?"*

*"You're quite correct, you <u>were</u> empty, but your ramp fell down just south of Birmingham. My pupil hit the accelerator instead of the brake. The rest is history ..."*

*"It's not usual to include supermarket visits in driving lessons Mrs. Henstooth ..."*

*"When you've been driving as long as I have, reversing becomes instinctive. Allow me to demonstrate."*

*"Excuse me dashing, but I simply must tell Daddy I've passed."*

*"Oops! Nearly missed that one!"*

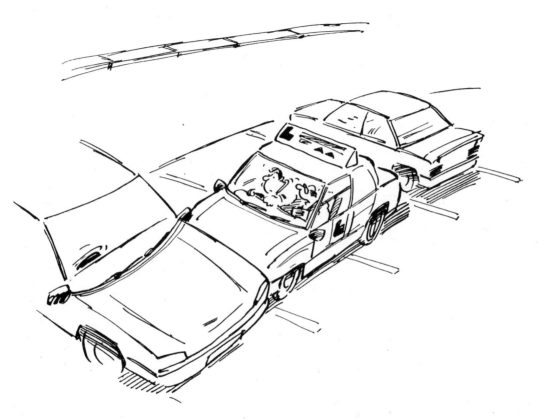

"I know you did it, but I don't know how."

*"This has significantly affected my chances of passing, hasn't it?"*

*"Oh no – it hasn't put me off at all – I regard it merely as a flat spot on the learning curve."*

*"So O.K. – The car's written off, but just think – if I hadn't swerved, we would have killed that squirrel!"*

*"I've been working on my emergency stops ..."*

*"Yes, yes – now don't forget to indicate if you decide to stop ..."*

*"It does that sometimes. Just keep a tight hold during the test."*

*"Oh Mr. Grimshaw! You're being far too masterful
with that gear lever!"*

*"You take this one – I want to watch his face."*

*"Oh no! I've failed already ..."*

"*Now the warden is telling you two things. One, you are parked in a restricted area, and two, the front offside wheel is resting on his foot.*"

*"Relax Mr. Pratt. It's not the end of the world –*
*just a very bad situation."*

"O.K. – big truck ahead – brake, change down – Hmm –
now where's that gear lever ...?"

*"You thought we were going to hit the truck,
didn't you, Mr. Ainsworth?"*

*"Yours, is he? I like a pupil with ambition ..."*

"If you'd care to step over here Mr. Fittock, let's see if you can read the number on that red car."

*"Ooh, great – a hill! I love hills."*

*"Just try to ignore the wipers, Mr. Pennington."*

*"Yes, I am a lady instructor. Do you have a problem with that?"*

*"Put my knee into gear one more time Mr. Farnswick,
and you'll walk home."*

*"Ooops! Well that's not reverse, is it?"*

*"Oh! That's reverse?"*

*"Power slides are not a compulsory test element Mr. Finch ..."*

*"Move over Mr. Fittock – I feel especially lethal today ..."*

"*I told you not to touch that!*"

*"The pictures are nice, but the story's a little disjointed ..."*

*"I said left!"*

*"This is a first for me, Purselove – how about you?"*

*"As I was about to say, 'before easing the car into reverse, check that the garage doors haven't swung shut."*

"'Driving school? Don't be silly,' you said.
'I'll teach her myself,' you said."

*"Mmm! It's good this! When do you think I should apply for my test, Dad?"*

"*Fathers teaching sons just doesn't work!
Why not let him go to a driving school?*"

"He's getting ready for tomorrow's lesson."

*"Driving lesson – five minutes ..."*

"You must come out now Mr. Farnsworth,
your examiner is waiting ..."

*"Wait! I've just thought of twenty-seven-thousand
things I'd rather do!"*

*"You've passed"*

*"Mmm! Want to go round again?"*

*"Mr. Harrison, Mr. Harrison, this horrid little man says I've failed!"*

*"This is cousin Leo and cousin Clint. They've come to cheer when I've passed."*

"There's one for every test I've failed ..."

*"Well? Did you pass, son?"*

## Books in the "Crazy World" series
($4.99 £2.99 paperback)

The Crazy World of Aerobics (Bill Stott)
The Crazy World of Cats (Bill Stott)
The Crazy World of Cricket (Bill Stott)
The Crazy World of Gardening (Bill Stott)
The Crazy World of Golf (Mike Scott)
The Crazy World of the Greens (Barry Knowles)
The Crazy World of The Handyman (Roland Fiddy)
The Crazy World of Hospitals (Bill Stott)
The Crazy World of Housework (Bill Stott)
The Crazy World of Learning (Bill Stott)
The Crazy World of Love (Roland Fiddy)
The Crazy World of Marriage (Bill Stott)
The Crazy World of The Office (Bill Stott)
The Crazy World of Photography (Bill Stott)
The Crazy World of Rugby (Bill Stott)
The Crazy World of Sailing (Peter Rigby)
The Crazy World of Sex (David Pye)

## Books in the "Mini Joke Book" series
($6.99 £3.99 hardback)

These attractive 64 page mini joke books are illustrated throughout by Bill Stott.

A Binge of Diet Jokes
A Bouquet of Wedding Jokes
A Feast of After Dinner Jokes
A Knockout of Sports Jokes
A Portfolio of Business Jokes
A Round of Golf Jokes
A Romp of Naughty Jokes
A Spread of Over-40s Jokes
A Tankful of Motoring Jokes

## Books in the "Fanatics" series
($4.99 £2.99 paperback)

The **Fanatic's Guides** are perfect presents for everyone with a hobby that has got out of hand. Eighty pages of hilarious black and white cartoons by Roland Fiddy.

The Fanatic's Guide to the Bed
The Fanatic's Guide to Cats
The Fanatic's Guide to Computers
The Fanatic's Guide to Dads
The Fanatic's Guide to Diets
The Fanatic's Guide to Dogs
The Fanatic's Guide to Husbands
The Fanatic's Guide to Money
The Fanatic's Guide to Sex
The Fanatic's Guide to Skiing

## Books in the "Victim's Guide" series
($4.99 £2.99 paperback)

Award winning cartoonist Roland Fiddy sees the funny side to life's phobias, nightmares and catastrophes.

The Victim's Guide to the Dentist
The Victim's Guide to the Doctor
The Victim's Guide to Middle Age

**Great Britain:** Order these super books from your local bookseller or from Exley Publications Ltd, 16 Chalk Hill, Watford, Herts WD1 4BN. (Please send £1.30 to cover postage and packing on 1 book, £2.60 on 2 or more books.)